LIVING THE MOMENT

IS THE FIRST STEP OF

A SACRED JOURNEY

FOR

My Darling
Clarence

Published by

The Thaler Corporation Inc.,

R. R. # 2, Alton,

Ontario, L0N 1A0,

CANADA

(519) 927-5213

CANADIAN CATALOGUING IN PUBLICATION DATA

Secretan, Lance H. K.
Living the moment: a sacred journey

ISBN 0--9694561-1-5

1.Vision quests-Fiction. 2.Indians, of North America-Canada-Religion and mythology-Fiction. 3.Indians of North America-Canada-Fiction. I. Title

PS8587. E37L58 1992 C813' . 54 C92-094852-9
PR9199. 3. S43L58 1992

Designed by Corporate Lines Design Group Inc.
Printed in Canada by Tri-Graphics Printing Ltd. on recycled paper
First printing - July 1992.

♻

Author's Note

During my research for **Living the Moment** I became aware of the concept of "cultural appropriation" - the assignment of a "Native voice" by a non-native. In writing **Living the Moment** I have attempted to capture the essence of Native North American myths, legends and traditions while deeply respecting them. Living the Moment is written in the spirit of love and friendship for <u>**all**</u> my Brothers and Sisters.

Illustrator's Note

The highly spiritual aspects of Native culture touches a deep chord within me. My inspiration for these illustrations was enriched by the work of the Haida and Sioux people.

Also by Lance Secretan

The Masterclass

The Way of the Tiger

Managerial Moxie

FOR

TRICIA

WHO LIVES EVERY MOMENT,

PASSIONATELY, NOBLY AND WITH LOVE

AND WHO LOVES LIFE AND PEOPLE AND

VERY FORTUNATELY,

ME.

LANCE H.K. SECRETAN

LIVING THE MOMENT

A Sacred Journey

Illustrated by Carolyn MacLeod Megill

In the Land of the Long Snows lived a wise chief whose name was Moon Bear. He was born under the Harvest Moon and was as strong as his great grizzly namesake. Chief Moon Bear had love in his heart and wisdom in his soul. His people revered him.

The chief had two sons, Sees-Like-a-Hawk and Sees-Like-an-Eagle and as in the Natural World, Hawk was Little Brother to Eagle. Moon Bear was an observant father, giving these names to his sons after noticing their differing outlooks on life. One, he discovered, had the viewpoint of the hawk while the other's perspective was more like that of the eagle. When hunting, the hawk sees the mouse and dives directly for it. But when the eagle hunts, he sees the panorama; detecting motion in that wider view, he dives, learning only later the nature of his prey. The hawk is guided by purpose, the eagle by skill.

One morning, Moon Bear called Hawk and Eagle to a family meeting.

"It is time for you to learn the lessons of Mother Earth," he told them. "It is your turn to master the message of the mountains; to listen to the songs of the plains, the sky, the forests and the rivers; to study the ways of the fish, the animals and, just as important, your Brothers and Sisters. During your Quest you will travel and live with different Clans, walking in their moccasins. When you are ready, you will continue your journey, finding new Brothers and Sisters from whom to learn. You will meet those who share our ways and some who do not; for those who wish to hear, there are insights to be gained from both."

"Remember to see like the hawk as well as the eagle. Live this way until the Spirit has spoken its secrets, to your hearts as well as your heads. When that Moment arrives you will know what you must know. This will be your signal to return here, for I shall then pass on to you leadership of our people."

Moon Bear gave them each a deerskin pouch in which he placed a large amethyst, the mineral totem of those born under the Harvest Moon. The amethyst is considered the symbol of judgment, patience and courage. In the pouch he also placed two palmfuls of crushed violets, the plant totem of the Harvest Moon, symbolizing health, humor and happiness. To the outside of each pouch, Moon Bear attached a purple feather from a mallard's wing. Purple, the totem color of the Harvest Moon, symbolizes inspiration, spiritual insight and creative power.

In this way, the Spirit of the Father would accompany his sons on their journey.

It was a day of mixed emotions for the great Chief, for he was proud of his sons but apprehensive, too; proud of their vigor and character, but anxious about the challenges that would greet them during their journey.

And he knew how much he would miss them for they were a great source of his joy.

The summer was in the spring as Hawk and Eagle set out on their Vision Quest.

The robins returned to the North, as they always do, and the Great Spirit used the valley as his painting canvas. When he was pleased with his work he called upon the Snow Spirit to erase the valley's varied hues. And this is how the Seasons passed.

Hawk and Eagle camped with the Rainbow Clan, a small, fun-loving group of young innocents who lived their lives with passion. The two Brothers became like bees in a flower garden, connecting with whatever interested them,

lighting on whatever could support them,
indulging themselves with whatever absorbed
them.They learned, they loved, they hunted and
they played, each as well as he could.

Sees-Like-a-Hawk was not humorless but
preferred introspection; he was a thinker
and dreamer: studious,

tightly focused and laconic. But more than any-thing, he was a hunter. He treasured his many solo trips for they enabled him to polish his skills, while being close to the Natural Things and his other Earth Relations. It was his time to give order to his thoughts and practice his craft.

Sees-Like-an-Eagle was more gregarious and, being bigger than his Brother, more physical. He was a formidable hunter, too, but unlike Hawk, it was not his passion. He would rather dance, entertain and make music than puzzle out the signs from the Spirits. He enjoyed action; he was expansive, full of mirth and energy and always ready for fun.

As the seasons passed, the two boys grew into inseparable friends. Like a bow and an arrow. Across the Land of the Long Snows, their hunting prowess became legendary. The two were known, simply, as Hawk and Eagle, the Great Hunters.

Hawk preferred the company of his closest friends. Eagle tended to be more social, always attracting new friends. Whenever the dance drum was brought out, both put on a display that even the Old Ones said had never been bettered. They were a delight to all.

Even to this day, when you walk past a stand of Quaking Aspens, you will see them shaking their leaves, laughing as they recall Hawk and Eagle's warm humor.

One evening Hawk and Eagle retreated to the high territory of their own minds and Spirits. As they brewed a delicate tea from the violet petals Chief Moon Bear had given them, they contemplated their future and reflected on the health, humor and happiness of the past. Although they loved their life with the Rainbow Clan, it seemed to lack purpose. They sensed that they had reached their potential here. It was time to move on. They explored their concerns and clarified their thoughts. They knew it was time to become more responsible, and they yearned to own fine things.

Magpie, who was eavesdropping in the willow above, flew down to a rock beside them.

"I belong to the Magpie Clan," he said to the two Brothers. "Why don't you join us? We would make you welcome and help you acquire possessions. We live far from here, near the Sweetgrass Hills, but I will gladly take you there."

The Father Sun framed Hawk and Eagle in a salmon sky. They listened eagerly to Magpie's stories about the fabulous riches awaiting the ambitious. Fantasies of wealth arose in their minds. As darkness fell, the forest was caressed by night's dewy embrace. The crickets and the nightbirds sang in conspiracy with Magpie as he seduced Hawk and Eagle with the force of his argument. The two Brothers resolved to join his tribe and become the best they could be.

The trio traveled many long days and nights as Magpie guided them through the great forests and mountain passes. Eventually, they arrived in the Land of Chattels.

Hawk and Eagle found the Magpie Clan very
different from the Rainbow Clan. The Magpie
Clan measured status by the number and worth
of their possessions, which they called "Chattels."
The most powerful member of the Clan was the
Chief, and he owned the greatest collection of
Chattels. The endless quest for more Chattels
wasn't easy, especially for the weak and young.
Some Clan members stole Chattels to keep pace
with the others. Some tried to impress their peers
by inventing tall tales about their Chattels. Some
people had no possessions at all. They became
outcasts.

Hawk and Eagle soon aspired to the wealth of
their new Brothers and Sisters. Often they would
lie awake deep into the night, talking excitedly
about the things they would own and sometimes
they would fall asleep dreaming of their future
riches. Their great hunting mastery, enabled them
to adapt easily to their new lifestyle. Hawk did not
yearn for a large collection of Chattels, wanting
only the very finest examples of each type.

Eagle, on the other hand, wanted it all and his appetite for more seemed to have no bounds. They soon learned to speak "Want," the language of the Magpie Clan, and they committed themselves to amassing the greatest treasury of possessions in the Clan's history.

Before many seasons had passed, the two had built a vast collection of Chattels. The elders had

never seen such wealth. Hawk and Eagle lived side by side in a private compound, in the two largest tepees in the land of Chattels. They kept many of their Chattels inside their tepee and, in accordance with the custom of the Magpie Clan, they hung others beside their Medicine Bundle on a wooden tripod that rose to the roof. A few of the small and most precious Chattels, particularly those they had acquired recently, were fastened to a buckskin thong and worn around their necks.

One day, Hawk and Eagle returned to their camp after a lengthy hunting and trapping expedition. They had brought home a heavy burden of new trophies. As they approached their tepees, they noticed Magpie flying away with one of Hawk's most prized possessions, a flute carved from the wing-bone of an eagle. As they entered their tepees they were faced with a terrible truth: all of their Chattels had been stolen. Hawk and Eagle leaped onto their horses and gave chase to the treacherous Magpie.

For three days and nights the two hunters stretched their tracking skills to the limit as they raced across the barren terrain. Without sleep or rest, they stayed as close to Magpie as a burr to a fetlock. They were a perfectly matched tracking team. Using his ability to focus, Hawk never let Magpie out of his sight, while Eagle used his wider vision to guide them safely through the unfriendly terrain.

Eventually Magpie led them to a cave in the farthest region of the Land of Chattels. Hawk and Eagle watched Magpie fly directly into the entrance, which was hidden beneath a crag overhanging a canyon. Immediately below them raged the rapids of the River of Chattels.

In the cave, heaped in every direction, were more Chattels than even the most covetous heart could imagine: moccasins, incense, hides and furs, paints, ornaments, beads, drums, medicine pipes and archery equipment. As the two pushed farther into the cave they saw jewelry, utensils, canoes, musical instruments, blankets, tobacco, food. Each section of the cave stretched into another as far as the eye could see. They even passed a section of stables that housed the finest appaloosas, skewbalds and palominos they had ever seen.

As they wandered past the treasures they could hear the cackling of an old man. It was Coyote-the-Old-Hoarder, who was prowling and patrolling his vast but lonely collection of Chattels - a joyless treasure he could share with no one because he had hoarded himself poor.

Hawk and Eagle were exhausted. They sat down in the entrance to the cave, propping their backs against the sun-baked rock-face. The ground shuddered from the rapids pounding below them.

"Coyote-the-Old-Hoarder has stolen all our Chattels and hidden them here. How shall we return them to our camp?" Eagle asked Hawk, venting his frustration.

Hawk, always the more reflective of the two, didn't reply. Instead, he reached for his buckskin pouch. Unwrapping the amethyst that Chief Moon

Bear had
given him, he
motioned to Eagle
to do the same. Though he
was only one year younger than
Eagle, under conditions like these he
often tended to assume the role of Elder.

They sat together in silence,

each rolling the smooth amethysts

in their calloused hands, drawing deeply on

their resources of judgment, patience and courage.

At last Hawk spoke. "Why?" he asked.

"Why what?" said Eagle, who by now had
forgotten his earlier question.

"Why shall we retrieve our Chattels and return
them to our tepees?"

Eagle paused. An answer did not readily pres-
ent itself. The longer Eagle mused, the more he
realized that a voice deep inside him had been
asking the same question. He recalled that some
of the Magpie Clan members were suspicious of

23

each other. It was difficult for them to tell who had attained Chattels by stealing, who had earned their Chattels and who were just pretending to have many Chattels.

"I've become disenchanted with Chattels," Hawk continued. "We are forever chasing and hunting, never savoring and enjoying. We spend our lives serving our own Spirit, never the Spirit of others.We have so much, and yet we are empty."

Eagle sympathized with Hawk's line of thinking. "We have become just like Coyote-the-Old-Hoarder and his helper, Magpie," he said.

"And like them," Hawk added, "we have become takers instead of givers." He rose and placed his hand on his Brother's shoulder, playing the role of Elder again. But his Brother didn't mind. "Let's leave the Land of Chattels before Coyote-the-Old-Hoarder steals our hearts, too, and adds them to his collection."

Hawk and Eagle surveyed the horizon and listened to the thunder of the rapids. They walked together to the edge of the crevasse and stared in wonder at the tangle of rocks below them. The song of the Water Spirit was telling them that they had become the best they could be with the Magpie Clan. It was time to continue their Journey.

Hawk and Eagle built a fire with a bow and spindle and talked into the night, Hawk responding to Eagle's exuberance with his usual taciturn commentaries. The wisps of cedar-smoke carried their thoughts up to the Sky Country.

"Let's abandon our Chattels - they have no real Meaning," said Hawk. "Even though we have lost them, we have lost nothing of ourselves. We are not our Chattels. It is we who are significant, not what we own."

"We will leave them to Coyote-the-Old-Hoarder," agreed Eagle. He jabbed the embers with a rotten twig and then threw it into the fire. "You are right about Chattels, Hawk. They have no Meaning. How can we learn about Meaning? Where do we find it?"

Hawk stood up to stretch and then sat down

again and crossed his legs. He loved his Brother very much. He often felt that they were simply one Spirit sharing two bodies. It made him feel whole to have such a good friend.

"Do you remember the story of the Turtle Clan that Moon Bear used to tell us?" he asked.

Eagle nodded.

"Tell it to me again," said Hawk.

Eagle prepared his thoughts as he poked the fire's embers again.

"A long time ago," he began, "the Great Spirit became sad at the way Earth's children were fighting, so he commanded the Water Spirits to cover the earth so that he could start again. Only the elements, a few plants and the swimming animals survived. But there was loneliness on Earth and the remaining animals yearned for the human companionship they had once enjoyed."

"In the Sky Country lived a Spirit Woman who was lonely, too. The animals wanted to invite her to join them, but she could not. There was no

land for her to walk on. So the animals met to ponder this dilemma. 'I have the answer,' offered Giant Turtle. 'I will raise my back out of the water and the Spirit Woman can come to the Earth and be on it.'

And so the Spirit Woman came and walked around her new home on Giant Turtle's back. Though she was grateful to Giant Turtle for his generosity, she was sad that he could no longer be with his family. So she asked all the animals to bring a little earth to put on Giant Turtle's back so that he could be free again to do Turtle things. Muskrat and Beaver organized the other animals and soon Giant Turtle's back was covered with earth. Then she said to Giant Turtle, 'As I breathe life into the earth, it will multiply. Then you may swim away to your family.'"

Hawk smiled admiringly at his Brother. They had both

heard this story many times, but Eagle told it better than anyone. Eagle relished this moment of unspoken praise.

Hawk took up the tale, finishing it for his Brother. "This generous act gave great Meaning to the life of Giant Turtle. In honor of his generosity, the Spirit Woman called that land Turtle Island. In time, all of Nature's other creatures returned, too. To this day it is where the Turtle Clan lives."

They sat quietly, staring into the flickering embers. A spark flew from the fire and vanished into the heavy quiet.

Eagle broke the silence. "Let's go there...let's travel to Turtle Island where we can be with the Turtle Clan. The Giant Turtle gave Meaning to his life and shared it with all his Earth Relations on Turtle Island. Let us join them and learn more about this Meaning."

Hawk and Eagle unrolled their blankets before kicking red earth into the fire. The night surrounded them and it was still. They were alone with the One-Who-Dwells-in-All-Places.

Hawk and Eagle rode for eight days and nights, making camp along the way, until they arrived at the Land of Many Springs. Their clothes were ragged. They rested in the High Woods at the forest's edge. Shards of light plunged through the canopy, splashing onto the damp moss of the forest floor.

Around the roots the water foamed. Hawk and Eagle quenched their thirst and rinsed their faces with the soft, sweet waters. The sounds of songbirds filled their ears and the springs seemed to rise all around them. The Water Spirits burbled, spluttered and splashed into streams which flowed down into the valley. It was a good land, a giving land.

As Hawk and Eagle led their horses into the stream, they splashed water onto the smooth rocks which had been warmed by the Father Sun, and plumes of steam rose from them. Shielding their eyes from the sky, they traced the course of the rapids, which fanned out into broad waters that flowed as far as the clouds could see. Hawk and Eagle peered into the farness, where the Heavens buffed the Earth. In the misted distance they could see the Great-Lake-Between-the-Mountains. Cradled in its center, like an eye-spot on the wing of a Silkworm Moth, was Turtle Island.

Following the teachings of Giant Turtle, the Turtle Clan lived a life dedicated to sacrifice and generosity. Many of their members were from other Clans - several were even former members of the Magpie Clan. All shared a common vision: a life beyond the mere acquisition of Chattels. Their preference was for a simpler style, dedicated more to doing things than wanting things. The result they called "Meaning."

Their work was of benefit to others; they created clothing, pottery, medicine and food. They shared themselves with their community.

Above all, Turtle Clan members did the things that would matter to others when they themselves had long passed into the world of Spirit. They sought to ensure that their children, families and friends would be proud of them and continue to remember them with kindness when they joined with the Sky People. They hoped that their short visit with Mother Earth would be filled with Meaning.

The Turtle Clan were healers and dreamers, working their Medicine with conviction. The stars, the weather and the terrain were their mentors. Every plant and berry had a healing purpose, and the Healing Spirits spoke through every living thing as they helped the Turtle Clan carry out their mission.

Hawk and Eagle used their mastery of hunting to develop greater Meaning in their lives. They shared with their Brothers and Sisters, their finesse in hunting and trapping. Often they gave their catch to the less experienced and fortunate. They spent much of their time coaching the most eager hunters to greatness.

Late one afternoon the sky suddenly darkened and Thunder came striding over the mountains. The Thunderbird threw fiery spears at the tallest trees. The Wind Spirits bent the sage and the flowers to the ground. Heavy rains bruised the earth. Even the strongest oaks submitted to the snarling storm. The children wept with the rains as the animals and birds deserted Turtle Island.

As dawn struck the ground a
stillness smothered the plain.
The halls of the forest were silent,
and the sky empty. The giant trees stood tall in
silent authority as Nature's abundance, so long
enjoyed by the Turtle Clan, became a memory.

The Old Ones, who were afraid of the omen,
sent a delegation to Hawk and Eagle. "Our lives
will have no Meaning if we cannot continue to
give," they said. "In order to give we must survive,
and we cannot survive without food. You are our
best woodsmen, our greatest hunters. Take our
finest canoe and anything else that you need,
and bring the animals back to us."

For Hawk and Eagle this represented the pinn-
acle of Meaning: their chance to become a living
legend of the Turtle Clan. The old Medicine
Woman prepared the food and moccasins they
would need for their long journey. The Clan's
most experienced hunters gave them their finest
hunting arrows, knives and decoys.

The Turtle Clan held a Sun Dance ceremony to
bless Hawk and Eagle's mission. Then they decorated the canoe with eagle plumes and buffalo
horns before slipping it quietly into the Great-
Lake-Between-the-Mountains.

Hawk and Eagle followed the golden path laid
for them on the water by the Moon Woman. Even
with the shore wind to help them they took two
days to reach the strand.

At last they arrived at the landing place, their
bodies aching for sleep. But
before they had taken

a step ashore they were greeted by the Wind Spirit. He would not let Hawk and Eagle rest until he spoke to them.

"I am sent by One Greater, to show you a different trail," he said. "I am the Wind. It is I, the Wind Spirit, who gives you each Moment. Each Moment of life depends on the Wind - even that which comes from your mouth. When the Wind ceases there will be no more Moments."

"What is our trail?" asked Eagle apprehensively.

"Your trail is the Moment," replied the Wind Spirit. "There is only one Great Thing - it is the Moment. It fills the world with light."

With these words, the Wind became still.

Though their mission was urgent, their body's cry for rest was too strong to resist. Hawk and Eagle slept under the stars of the Dipper which they knew as the Wolf Road and the Seven Wolves.

Something awakened Hawk. Slowly, he adjusted his eyes to the dawn. Something was pressing gainst his leg. Before he could reach for his knife he heard the unmistakable buzz of the Rattlesnake. Suddenly he felt very cold.

"What's the matter?" asked Eagle, sitting up suddenly.

His question was answered instantly by the Rattlesnake, who buzzed his tail again. Hawk and Eagle were as still as stone.

"I am sent by One Greater, to teach you another Way," the Rattlesnake told them. "I am Life or Death. It is I, the Spirit of Fate, who gives you each Moment. At any Moment you may be chosen. When the Spirit of Fate chooses to steal your breath there will be no more Moments."

The Rattlesnake slid across the grass, merging into the mist.

"What is this Moment about which the Spirits speak?" asked Eagle.

"If we do no not know what we are looking for,

we will be unable to understand what we find,"
said Hawk. "Let us consider these things."

They moved with the deliberation and calmness
of those who are one with all their Earth Relations
and the Natural Things. Eagle decided to make a
totem. First he found a moss-covered rock which
resembled the face of a raven, which he believed
would help them

find the animals from Turtle Island because the
Raven is the symbol of balance between nature
and man and the harbinger of game. On the rock
he placed the mallard's wing-feather given to him
by Chief Moon Bear, for purple symbolizes inspiration, spiritual insight and creative power. Then
he wrapped the rock and the feather in a piece
of buckskin and placed the bundle between
the two of them.

Meanwhile, Hawk had collected some dry twigs and started a small fire, on which he placed sweet-grass. They sat beside it and savored the fragrance of the burning grass. And they traveled to the Big Sky of their minds.

"Is Meaning an illusion?" asked Eagle. "At first Meaning felt like giving, but is it really just another form of taking?" He passed the totem to Hawk.

Hawk nodded thoughtfully. "The eulogies, the praise, the appreciation, the gratitude, the testimonials - even the epitaph at the end of life - perhaps they are all simply more Chattels to be acquired," he said.

In the haste of life, Hawk and Eagle seldom found opportunities to philosophize this way. They moved only to pass the totem between them. Neither of them was ready to speak. Occasionally the quiet darkness was betrayed by the eruption of a twig delivering itself to the flames.

Finally, Eagle said, "When we camped with the Magpie Clan, we lived to acquire material things. Then when we camped with the Turtle Clan, we lived to acquire intangible things."

"Yes, we are confusing the destination with the journey," said Hawk, his thoughts were crystallizing. "If we direct our hearts to perfecting each step of the journey we shall arrive safely at our destination. The journey is the Moment."

"Let us test this wisdom," said Eagle. "Let us make this a great Moment."

As Hawk and Eagle were living the Moment, calmness and beauty caressed their shoulders, lifting the stress accumulated during the seasons they had spent with the Rainbow, Magpie and Turtle Clans. The most important thing at this instant in their lives was the quality of this Moment. Of this relationship. Of this task. Of this emotion. And of this thought. In this Moment one criterion eclipsed all others: that this discrete Moment of life should be invested with passion, making it the best that it could be.

And so the Questors received their Vision, and the lessons became clear. The message of the Wind Spirit and the Rattlesnake was fresh in their hearts: Every Moment is a privilege.

Eagle put words to their discovery. "With each Clan we have attempted to be the best we could be: having more fun than anyone else in the Rainbow Clan; acquiring more Chattels than anyone else in the Magpie Clan; giving more in order to achieve greater Meaning than anyone else in the Turtle Clan. Each step of our journey has led us to one goal only to achieve another."

"The Great Spirits have given us no law demanding that we excel at everything, that we should be better than everyone else," observed Hawk. "Nor has Chief Moon Bear made this demand of us. Yet the Spirit of Greed darkens our hearts and urges us all to do so."

Hawk looked at his Brother. "Perhaps the acquisition of Chattels, of status, prestige or recognition, will become irrelevant if we live the Moment," he said. "Perhaps this is our trail; this is the lesson from our Vision Quest that we must take home to Moon Bear."

"Perhaps, too," said Eagle, "a beautiful paradox

will flow from this discovery, because it is entirely possible that when we are living the Moment with passion, it will yield these rewards anyway - as inevitable as the ripening of an apple."

"Let us see if it is so," said Hawk.

The waters lapped the rocks which fringed the lake, and an unseen musician played in the roof of the forest. Hawk and Eagle swayed and chanted quietly to the Dawn as the embers warmed their souls. Though the mountains beckoned through the sunrise, the plateau was enough. Their hearts were intoxicated with the Moment.

In that sacred Moment Hawk noticed a frog sitting at his feet. This frog was like no other he had seen before. It was dressed in scarlet from head to toe.

"Greetings, Brother," said the frog, staring at Hawk.

"It is time for us to find the animals and return them to Turtle Island," said Eagle, unaware of

Hawk's encounter.

"Wait," Hawk said to him. "Look at this frog."

Eagle scanned the ground. "It is very color-ful, but we have an urgent task before us," he said, impatiently.

Hawk caught Eagle's shirt, pulling him back to his side. "We agreed to live the Moment," he reminded his Brother.

"Good Morning, little Sister," he said addressing the frog.

"I am called Jumps-High-From-the-Water," replied the frog. "I am in need of your Medicine."

"We are on an urgent mission, and time is against us," said Eagle.

"But this Moment is important to me, and I need your Medicine," pleaded Jumps-High-From-the-Water. "Please be with me and live in my Moment instead of your future."

Hawk and Eagle remembered their pledge. "What Medicine can we share with you?" Eagle asked the frog.

"Because I am so red, the big fish, the herons and the snakes can easily find me and this makes me afraid. And because the bugs and flies can easily see me, too, they run away before I can catch them. I have been hiding since the Cornplanting Moon, but if I was the same color as this mud on which we stand, they would not be able to see me."

"Then how can we assist you?" asked Eagle.

"If you pick up a handful of mud and sprinkle it on me, I will be disguised, "said Jumps-High-From-the-Water.

Hawk pried loose a piece of turf from the ground and shook the dirt that fell from its roots over the frog.

"Oh! Thank you!" she said, but her gratitude could only be heard, not seen, for Jumps-High-From-the-Water had merged with the mud.

Eagle turned to his Brother. "We must leave now and complete our mission," he said, and they packed their blankets and headed for the trail that led to the Strong Woods.

"I will travel with you," said Jumps-High-From
-the-Water.

Hawk and Eagle were sure that the animals
from Turtle Island were sheltering in the Strong
Woods. As they reached the forest's edge, they
heard a cry from Jumps-High-From-the-Water.
Turning, they saw that she had become visible
again: brown contrasting against green as she
stood in the middle of a moss patch.

"Now I can be seen again - please share your
Medicine once more with me," she pleaded.

"What would you like us to do now?"
asked Hawk.

"Crush the leaves of Water Cress and Marsh
Marigolds, and then sprinkle them over me."

As soon as Hawk and Eagle had done so,
Jumps-High-From-the-Water became invisible
again. As Hawk and Eagle traveled deeper into
the Strong Woods, she croaked, just to let them
know that she was still with them. But when they
came to the rapids, Jumps-High-From-the-Water
became a green frog in the white foam and was

afraid again. She implored the two Brothers to share their Medicine once more.

"Little Sister," said Hawk, "we cannot keep stopping to help you. Before the Moon Woman lights the Sky Country, we must find all of the animals of Turtle Island and return them."

"Trust me," said Jumps-High-From-the-Water with urgency. "Live with me in this Moment. Help me by scooping up some foam from the eddies and sprinkling it over me."

Hawk and Eagle did as Jumps-High-From-the-Water asked, and she immediately became one with the swirling waters. The two Brothers peered into the whirlpools, but she could not be seen. Suddenly she leaped out of the rapids and landed on the grassy bank - and became green. Then she jumped onto a tree stump and became brown. And then she jumped back into the water again and became invisible.

"Now it is my turn to live in your Moment, big Brothers," she said, as she jumped back out of the water. "I asked you to trust me and you did.

Now I will repay you with my Medicine. How can I assist you in this Moment?"

"We are here to find all of the animals that came from Turtle Island and help them to return to our Brothers and Sisters of the Turtle Clan," replied Eagle.

Jumps-High-From-the-Water held Council with the beavers. She persuaded them to build a lodge of aspen branches which would float on the Great-Lake-Between-the-Mountains, support-ing all of the animals for their journey back to Turtle Island. The Water Spirits were at peace, and this created ideal conditions for the beavers to complete their work. On the third day, all the animals were invited to assemble on the lodge, and the beavers, muskrats, otters and all the other swimming creatures towed them to Turtle Island.

And Jumps-High-From-the-Water went to live on Turtle Island, too.

Hawk and Eagle were relieved. This was the first time they had placed their faith in the Moment. They had done so with some trepidation. But they had been rewarded; their Natural Friends were safely returning to their home on Turtle Island.

"It is time for us to return to Chief Moon Bear," said Hawk.

In the Sky Country the Moon Woman permitted herself to smile.

The Old Chief strode briskly towards Hawk and Eagle, holding his right arm high in a Peace Salute. The purple bandana hanging loosely around his neck matched the amethysts which decorated his ears. He was a tall, strong man, imposing in his buckskin leggings, shirt and apron.

"Welcome home, my sons!" he said, proudly wearing tears on his leathered cheeks. He embraced them both in silent gratitude, aching with joy, holding them both so tightly to his chest that he could feel their beating hearts. His mouth was dry and his voice trembled. Holding them even tighter, he closed his eyes and thanked the

Spirits for returning his boys safely. "Tell me what

you have learned on your Journey," he asked

them softly as he released his grip.

Eagle spoke for them both. "We have spent

many Seasons listening to our Brothers and

Sisters, our other Earth Relations and the Natural Things. They have taught us that every Moment of Life is sacred and that each is to be honored - with an open mind and a closed mouth. The past is to be respected as greatly as the future and so we must consider the implications of every decision we make, on the seven generations that have gone before us and the seven that will follow. And in doing so we must live the Moment, for it is the Moment that must be lived." Eagle paused, and looking first at Moon Bear and then at his Brother, he added deliberately, "Every Moment is a privilege."

"And when you give yourself to the Moment, it will reward you generously," said Hawk. "Life gives to the giver and takes from the taker."

Chief Moon Bear was happy through his tears. A smile flared across his face, like a sunrise, radiating pride and love.

"You are wise to have discovered that when you give yourself to the Moment, you are not living in the Moment, nor are you living *for* the Moment,

you are simply *living the Moment* - nobly, passionately and with love. And every Moment deserves
everything you have to give."

Moon Bear cupped his big hands around each
of his sons' heads, holding their faces close to his.
He hugged them closely again and placed a kiss
on each of their foreheads. He looked to the Sky
People and thanked the Great Spirits for their
Wisdom, for he knew he would not see another
Harvest Moon before joining them.

But for now he would live this Moment, nobly,
passionately and with love.

This book is available at a special discount when ordered in
bulk quantities. A dramatized audio-cassette version is also
available. For more information about these and other products,
please contact:

Special Sales Department,
The Thaler Corp. Inc.,
Alton, Ontario, L0N 1A0,
CANADA.

Telephone: (519) 927-5213
Fax: (519) 927-3909